Liz Doolittle

MURDER & MISTERY SHORT STORIES

© 2020 by Liz Doolittle
© 2020 by UNITEXTO

Published by UNITEXTO

TABLE OF CONTENTS

FINDING ELLA

It had been 2 days since 14 year old Ella Sanderson had gone missing. The Police were looking for her. Ella was the 5th girl that had gone missing in the same month in their small town. The Police had no idea as to where the girls could have gone. Ben, Ella's 20 year old brother, was sat on Ella's bed in her room at the moment. He looked disturbed. It had been two days since his sister had gone missing. Their parents were really upset and Ben could do nothing to comfort them. He looked around the room, calling back Ella's memories. She was a bright child and Ben loved her very much. Ben's eyes found the doll sitting on Ella's bed. It was the same doll Ben had bought Ella on her 14th birthday last week. Ben picked it up. His eyes filled with tears. The girls that had gone missing before had not come back and Ben feared that Ella might never be coming back either. Suddenly, looking at the doll, Ben's eyes went wide in shock. He put the doll back and went outside. He took out his cell phone and called a number.

"Danielle, I need to see you right now," he said into the phone and headed out.

Officer Danielle Corcoran was Ben's childhood friend. He was looking into the case of missing girls. Ben and Danielle were sitting in a café.

"So, you're saying you found a camera in the doll's eyes. And now you want me to look in to the other missing girls' toys," Danielle summarized after listening to Ben.

"Yes, exactly. I think they might have cameras too and it all might be related. I think the person who have them was keeping an eye on them through the cameras" Ben explained.

"It's worth a try," Danielle said as his eyes brightened.

Danielle went to Myra's room in her house. Myra was the girl who had gone missing before Ella. He started to look among her toys. He kept looking for an hour but didn't find any toy with a camera in it. Danielle went to Myra's mother.

"Is there any chance Myra could have any other toys besides these?" He asked her, pointing to the toys all around Myra's room.

"That's pretty much it," she replied. "Oh, there is one more." She said remembering something. Danielle looked at her with interest. "I was missing her so I took her teddy bear with me to my room," she said in a sad voice as she directed Danielle to another room. A big teddy bear sat on the bed. Danielle went forward and picked it up. He looked closely and indeed, there was a camera in the bear's eye.

It went the same way with all the other missing girls' toys. Every girl had a toy that had a camera in its eye. And all of those toys had been recently bought.

"You know of the shop where you bought the doll for Ella?" Danielle asked Ben. They were back in the same café.

"Yes, I do," Ben answered.

"I think all those toys might be from the same shop," Danielle said.

"Let's go find out then," Ben said forcefully.

"No, you can't. I'll go alone," Danielle said to him.

"No, I'm going with you," Ben said with finality. Danielle couldn't stop him.

Danielle asked the parents of other missing girls and found out that the toys had been bought from the same shop. They reached the shop and went to the owner. The owner was an old man. Danielle handed him the list of the toys.

"These toys had been bought from your shop, right?" Danielle asked. The old man looked at the list.

"Yes, yes they were," the man replied. "But, why do you ask?"

"We need to know where they came from. Who made them?" Danielle asked again as he showed the man his card.

"Oh, you are Police," the man said as he realized. "I don't actually know who made them. There was this man who came to me with a truck full of toys. He asked me to buy them from him. He sold a lot cheaper so I bought them from him. Is there something wrong with the toys?" Ben and Danielle looked at each other. They told the man of the cameras in the toys. He was totally surprised.

"Look, we need you to try and remember anything you can about him, alright?" Ben said to him. The man was really worried now.

"He actually called me yesterday to ask if I needed more toys. I said Yes. He said he'll come the next day. So, he might come today," he told them. Ben and Danielle exchanged a look.

"Alright. We'll wait here in the shop. You just have to give us a look when he comes and we'll know," Danielle said to the old man.

"Okay," the man agreed.

So, they waited. An hour or so passed when a middle aged man dressed in black jeans and shirt entered the shop. He wore black cap so his face was half hidden. The owner looked towards them where they were hiding and they knew it was him. The man and the owner talked for about 5 minutes and then the man started out. He entered into his truck and drove. Ben and Danielle followed.

The man drove for about half an hour before he came to a stop in front of a house. He got out of the truck and entered the house. Ben and Danielle waited for a few moments. Then they went and rang the bell. No one answered at first. They rang 3 times more. At last, the man opened the door and looked at them with dislike.

"Who are you?" He asked flatly.

"Sir, we need to talk to you," Danielle said as he showed him his Police card. The man tried to shut the door at once but Ben caught him by the arm. The man fought him until Danielle finally pinned him to the ground.

"Where have you kept my sister?" Ben asked him angrily. The man just laughed. Ben and Danielle tied the man to a chair and searched his house. The found a door that led to a secret door. It was locked. The broke the lock and found all five girls in there. Ben looked until he found Ella and happiness filled him as he ran to her.

A STORY OF TWO SISTERS

Their parents had been found hanging from the fan. The Police had found nothing out of the order about the case. Therefore, they had come to the result that Richard and Molly had killed themselves. But, 15 year old twins, Lucy and Mira, did not believe that their parents killed themselves. They were not that kind of people who could have killed themselves, leaving their 15 year old daughters all by themselves. The four of them had been one happy family. How could they go ahead and destroy it all by their own hands?

But The Police did not agree with Lucy and Mira. Since both of them were underage, they were handed over to a distant cousin of their father who was the only living relative they had and who they had seen only once in their lives. So both of them packed their belongings and went to live with their uncle, Sam and his wife, Liz.

Sam and Liz were very nice to the girls and treated them very kindly. It had been a month since Lucy and Mira had come to live with their uncle. Sam and Liz were really nice but the girls still had not been able to get over the death of their parents. Mira was the quiet kind who thought about things a lot. Lucy was the strong kid who always took care of her twin sister. Together, the girls were trying to overcome the loss of their parents. They had started school again and were trying to get back to their lives.

One afternoon, Lucy was walking towards her room when she passed by her uncle's bedroom. The door was open a little and she could hear her uncle and aunt talking in low voices.

"This is the best thing we have ever done for ourselves," Liz was saying. Lucy went to the door to listen what they were talking about.

"You're right. If I knew life could be this much better, I would have killed Richard and Molly years ago," Sam replied. Lucy thought she had heard wrong.

"Yes, now we just have to get rid of the girls," Liz said. Lucy could not hear any longer. She ran back to her room. Mira was studying on her desk when Lucy entered the room, out of breath.

"What happened to you?" Mira asked her. Lucy looked as though she had seen a snake.

"We have to get out of here," Lucy said to her in a hurry.

"What do you mean?" Mira got up and reached her sister.

"It's them," Lucy started, her voice full of fear. "They killed Mom and Dad."

"Who are you talking about?" Mira asked, confused and surprised.

"Sam and Liz," Lucy replied in a low voice.

"What? That can't be," Mira could not believe it. "You must have heard wrong."

"No. I heard them talking just now. They were saying they would kill us too," Lucy said frightfully.

"But why would they do that?" Mira was still finding it difficult to understand.

"Simple," a voice said behind them. Lucy and Mira forgot to take breath. They slowly turned. Sam and Liz were standing in the doorway.

"Money, girls. Money," Liz said.

"Your father had a lot of money. And as you girls are not of age yet, you had to be moved to us. Along with the money," Sam said with a smile.

"But this was not how it should have gone. You were not to know of this until we killed you too," Liz added.

"And got all the money to ourselves." They were both completing each other's sentences. The girls were just standing there, unable to move, not sure what to think.

"Yeah. So you girls are to be locked in here until we sort out what to do with you now. Alright?" Liz said, smiling widely at them.

"Be good, girls. Stay quiet or we'll have to think of something else," Sam said as he went to the table and picked out the two cell phones of the twins. Then, they both got out and locked the door.

What now?" Mira asked Lucy through tears. She had been crying ever since Sam and Liz had locked them both in the room. Lucy had just gone quiet. Suddenly, she remembered something.

"Mira, do you still have the small burner phone that Mom and Dad had given us to use in times of any problems?" She asked Mira. Mira did not understand at first. Then.......

"Oh, that," she started as she understood. "Yes, I do." She went to her bag and pulled out a small phone from a secret pocket inside.

"I hope it has some battery left. I've switched it off ever since," she said as she handed the phone to Lucy. Lucy took it and turned it on.

"It has free minutes, right?" Lucy asked as the phone came to life.

"Yes," Mira replied. Lucy smiled as she called Officer Anderson's number.

Fifteen minutes later, Lucy and Mira heard the sounds of Police cars stopping in front of the house and a few minutes later, they heard the lock of their door opening. Officer Anderson was standing outside. He gave them a smile.

"That was a really smart move, Lacy. Remembering my number by heart," he said as he took the girls outside. Lucy managed a small smile.

THE JEWELS

Alex knew he was late when his car stopped in front of Lizzy's school. He got out and went to pick her up. Lizzy wasn't waiting by the door. He asked the watchman to call for her. The watchman came back a few minutes later and told him that the children had all already left. Alex got worried at once. He went inside and searched the school himself but the school was empty. There were no children at all. Alex was losing his mind. Where could Lizzy have gone? Alex could not even think of losing Lizzy. She was the only family he had and he loved her with all his heart.

When an hour had passed and he still couldn't find her, Alex decided to go to the Police. He got into his car and started it. Just then, his cell phone rang. Unknown number calling. He picked up.

"If you want your daughter alive, you must do what we ask of you," a heavy voice said from the other side. Alex forgot to breathe.

"Who are you?" He started. "What have you done to Lizzy?" He shouted.

"Oh, Lizzy is fine right now. But she won't be if you keep shouting like that," the voice replied calmly. Alex stopped.

"What do you want?" He asked slowly.

"We need you to do something for us," the voice started explaining.

It had been 3 hours since Lizzy had been brought to this place. There was a black covering on her eyes. They hadn't taken it off of her eyes. A few minutes ago, she had heard them talk to her Dad, asking him to steal some very expensive jewels from someone. They had provided him the address. Lizzy knew her father would do it. He loved her so much that he would give his own life to save her. She knew he won't involve the Police either as these people had told him that if he did, they would kill Lizzy. She just had to wait now.

Alex was going to steal the jewels. He was standing in front of a very big house. The people who had Lizzy had given him this address. Alex straightened his cap and went towards the house. He would do anything to save Lizzy.

Lizzy was a smart kid. Even though she couldn't see at the moment, she was using her other senses. She was getting this odd feeling that she knew this place. There was something that felt familiar to her. But she hadn't yet been able to understand what it was. The smell of the wood was trying to remind her of something but she hadn't yet caught what it was. Also, she noticed that the man and the woman tried to change their voices whenever they spoke to her. It was like they didn't want her to recognize them. Suddenly, a train passed by outside and a clear picture entered Lizzy's head. The sound of the train and the smell of the wood combined brought back a memory to her. She had been to this place before.

And at that moment, Lizzy knew where she was.

2 hours later, she heard them talk to Alex. She could even recognize their voices now. Then, one of them came to her.

"Your father got the jewels," it was the woman. She was trying to talk in a different voice but Lizzy knew who it was.

"Let's go," the man said and Lizzy recognized his voice too. They helped her to her feet and took her with them to the car.

Half an hour later, the car stopped. One of them got out while the other stayed with Lizzy. Lizzy heard Alex's voice in the distance. A few moments later, the man came back to the car and helped Lizzy out. He must have gotten his jewels from Alex. He walked Lizzy a few steps and then turned and went back to the car. Lizzy heard the car start and leave.

"Lizzy?" She heard Alex's voice. Lizzy removed her covering from her eyes and saw Alex standing there with a black covering on his eyes too. Of course they had made him wear it too so he won't recognize them.

"Dad," Lizzy said as she went to her father. He removed his cover and took her in his arms.

"Are you alright, sweetie?" Alex asked, worried.

"I know who they are," Lizzy replied. Alex just looked at his daughter.

"Who?" Alex asked slowly.

"It was Liam's parents," Lizzy said slowly. Liam was their neighbor and Lizzy's friend.

"What?" Alex said confused.

"Yes, they had taken me to their farm house but they didn't know that Liam had taken me and some other friends there once. The sound of the train and the smell of the wood was just the same. I recognized their voices too after that," Lizzy explained.

"Are you sure?" Alex asked her.

"A hundred percent," Lizzy said determinedly.

All they had to do now was leave a nameless tip with the Police from a public telephone about where the stolen jewels might be.

THE MYSTERIOUS DEATH IN ROOM 20

It was 07:00 in the morning when Jack woke up. The others were still asleep. It was a big room of their college hostel that he shared with 3 other boys. Jack got up and went to the attached bathroom. He came out 30 minutes later, drying his wet hair with a towel. He passed by Andy's bed and stopped dead. Andy's face was white as death.

"Andy, are you alright?" Jack asked him. Andy didn't reply. Jack tried to wake him up but Andy's head just turned to one side lifelessly. Jack fell back. He ran to wake Malcolm and Peter. They looked at him with empty eyes.

"Guys, wake up. There is something wrong with Andy," Jack shouted at them.

"When is there anything right with him?" Peter said and just turned on his side. Malcolm put his hands on his eyes.

"No, guys. He is not moving," Jack shouted again. Malcolm and Peter sat up in their beds and looked at Andy. He was still lying on his bed. They got up and moved to him. They saw his white face and their eyes went wide.

Andy was dead.

The Police were called immediately. An empty glass of juice lay on Andy's side table. Andy's body had been taken and it was found that his blood and the glass of juice contained strong amounts of sleeping tablets. It seemed someone had put the sleeping tablets in Andy's juice. But the real question was, who?

It was just four boys in the room. The thing was that the room had been locked from the inside. And there was no other door. That meant that no one from the outside could have come to do the dirty thing. It had to be one of the three boys. Or was it all of them combined? The two Officers named Perkins and Evans were called in to find the answers to these questions.

The three boys sat in front of the two Police Officers. They looked at the three of them closely.

"I want you three to tell me everything that happened in detail," Perkins asked. So Jack started to explain from the point he had woken up. When he had finished, Perkins looked towards Malcolm and Peter.

"Is this true?" He asked them.

"Yes," the replied together. "I mean from the point we woke up," Malcolm added. Jack looked towards Malcolm in surprise.

"Right. So, that means Jack was the only one awake before you two," Perkins said.

"What is that supposed to mean?" Jack started. "Do you think I killed Andy?"

"I didn't. You are the one who said that," Perkins said calmly. Jack just looked at him.

"All right. We came to know that none of you actually liked Andy. Is that right?" Evans asked this time. The three boys looked at each other.

"That is not true," Peter said.

"But we have heard from other students that you guys were fighting with Andy most of the time," Evans added.

"We did not fight with him. We just told him to keep himself and the room clean. He was always throwing his clothes and shoes around the room and not caring about cleaning up. That made us uncomfortable since we shared the room with him," Malcolm explained.

"Right. We'll need to question you again later. You can leave now," Evans said as he let them go.

The three boys had stopped talking to one another. Everyone seemed to think the other might be the killer. Even the other students were not talking to the three of them and Jack noticed that they were afraid of them. Only Emily, Jack's girlfriend, was the one who talked to him and believed him. He was so thankful to her for that. But Jack knew that the fact that he was the first one to wake up that day was putting him in a difficult position. Even the Police seemed to think that he might have killed Andy. And the strange thing was that the room had been locked from the inside. They had never kept the room locked when they were inside. Why was it locked that day, then?

He was think about all of this when Amber, Andy's only friend, came to him.

"Jack, can I talk to you?" She asked him. Jack didn't remember ever interested in talking to her. She seemed so sad. There were big dark circles around her eyes. Jack had never seen her in such a bad condition.

"Yes, sure," he said as he moved to make place for her on the bench.

"She sat down. Jacked looked at her. She seemed to be trying to find words to say. And after a few moments...

"It's nothing. I'm sorry," she said in a low voice, got up quickly and left. Jack just watched her go.

Police Officers Perkins and Evans had called for them again. This time, they had talked to all of them separately. They seemed to think the three of them had killed Andy together. They told all three of them separately to admit to it before one of the other does. That would reduce the punishment of the one who admits first. None of them admitted to it.

Jack was sat on the bench again, thinking about all of this. He felt as if he was missing something. Something that was right at the corner of his mind, but every time he came close, it disappeared. And then, something came to his mind

"You'll all be sorry for this," a voice sounded in his head. And then it all started to make sense. The locked room, the juice, Amber behaving confused and afraid. Jack got up excitedly. He knew what he had to do.

Jack found Amber in an empty classroom, crying her eyes out.

"Are you alright?" He asked her. Amber jumped and turned around.

"Oh, yes. I'm fine," she replied, drying her eyes. Jack went and sat with her. None of them spoke for a while. And then..............,

"He killed himself, didn't he?" Jack said slowly. Amber looked at him in surprise and then she started crying.

"I tried to stop him. He wouldn't listen. He wasn't stable at his mind. He wanted to punish you guys too for behaving badly to him. So, he planned all this," Amber said through tears. Jack put a hand on her shoulder and tried to comfort her.

The mystery was solved at last.

AMANDA STARK IS DEAD

It had been a few hours since Amanda Stark's body had been found in the river by a group of three boys in a boat. There were angry red marks on her neck. The body had already been sent for tests to be performed to understand the exact cause of her death. Police Officers Fred Nilsson and Ryan Rogers were present at Amanda's home with her family. A middle aged woman was sitting on the sofa with a middle aged man. They looked to be Amanda's parents. The woman was crying hard and the man had his arm around her shoulders, trying to comfort her. Officer Nilsson cleared his throat.

"We are really sorry for your daughter, Mr. and Mrs. Stark," he said slowly. Mr. Stark raised his head and looked at him. His eyes were red as blood. He must have been crying a lot. He didn't say anything.

"We'd like to ask a few questions about Amanda," Nilsson went on. Mr. Stark moved his head slowly in confirmation.

"I'm William Stark. This is my wife, Tina," he said looking in the woman's direction, "and that's my eldest son, Tom and his wife, Mia." He pointed to another sofa where a man in his early thirties was sitting with a woman who looked quite close to his age. Mia had a baby in her arms who seemed to be a few months old.

"Amanda has a twin sister too, right?" Officer Nilsson asked.

"Yes. Alicia will be joining us shortly," replied Mr. Stark.

"Okay, alright. So, tell us about Amanda. When did you guys last see her?" Officer Rogers asked this time.

"We saw her yesterday morning at breakfast." Mr. Stark's voice was slow and heavy. "But, I went to office after that and that was the last time I saw her." Rogers turned his head to Tom and Mia.

"What about you guys?" He asked them.

"I went to office with Dad. I didn't see her after that." Tom replied.

"Actually, none of us saw her after breakfast. She left home after that and didn't even come home at night," Mia added.

"Did she do that quite often? Not sleeping at home I mean?" Nilsson asked no one in particular.

"Yes." Mrs. Stark spoke for the first time. "Yes, she did. She often went to her boyfriend's to stay. So we thought she might be with Jamie." Nilsson and Rogers looked at each other.

"Amanda had a boyfriend?" Nilsson asked.

"Yes." A voice came from behind them. A young girl with black hair came and sat on a chair. "Yes, she did. Jamie Watson. He goes to College with us." She added.

"This is Alicia. Amanda's twin sister," Mr. Stark said. Nilsson and Rogers looked at her. Alicia looked a lot like Amanda. She looked as though she had just woken up.

"Right. So, did she behave any different yesterday morning? Was she worried or afraid or something like that?" Rogers asked, looking at all of them one by one. Everyone seemed to think for a while.

"No, I don't think so," replied Mr. Stark. Everyone seemed to agree.

"Amanda said she was going to meet Jamie yesterday," Alicia said suddenly. Nilsson and Rogers sat up straight and then exchanged a look.

Nilsson and Rogers were sat on a couch in Jamie's sitting room with Jamie sitting in front of them. He looked to be around 20 years old. Same as Amanda.

"So, Jamie," started Nilsson, "When did you meet Amanda yesterday?"

"Umm, at around lunch time, I guess" Jamie replied. "We had lunch and spent the afternoon watching TV here. She left in the evening and that was the last time I ever saw her." He had a pained look in his eyes.

"Did she say where she was going?" Rogers asked him.

"No, not exactly. But I thought she must be going home," Jamie replied.

"Okay, Jamie. We'll call you if we have any more questions for you," Nilsson said and they both got up and left.

Police Officers Nilsson and Rogers were sitting in their office drinking coffee and going through some files.

"What do you think of Jamie, Ryan?" Nilsson asked. Officer Rogers looked up.

"I'm not sure. But you already know that in most cases, it's always the boyfriend," Rogers replied. Nilsson thought for a while.

"What do you think could be the reason?" Nilsson asked again.

"For Jamie to kill Amanda? I don't know. May be they fought. May be she tried to break up with him and he got angry. Could be anything." Rogers explained. Nilsson didn't say anything.

Alicia was going to her room when she heard the baby crying. She went to Tom and Mia's room. They weren't there and the baby was lying on the bed, crying. She went and picked him up. He stopped crying and fell asleep after a few moments. She lay him on bed again. She was going to return to her room when she saw the family photo on the wall. She looked at Amanda smiling and looking happy with her family. Alicia went to the wall and as soon as she touched Amanda's face on the photo, something fell down from behind the photo. Alicia bent down and picked it up. It was a diary. She opened it and saw Amanda's name on it. Confused, she opened the diary from the middle.

I saw Tom with a girl today. I asked him about who she was but he didn't give any serious answer.

Alicia turned another page.

Tom was again with that same girl again. I found out that she was his secretary. I pushed Tom and he told me that he liked her. I told him to end it or I'll tell our family.

Alicia was really confused now. She kept turning pages.

Tom is not giving up that girl. I have no choice but to tell Mia and my parents. This cannot go on forever. I'll tell them tonight.

The next pages were empty. This was the last sentence. Alicia looked at the date. It was the same day Amanda had died.

"Oh my God." Alicia said to herself in disbelief. "This can't be." Just then, there was a sound. Alicia turned and saw Tom standing in the doorway.

"What are you doing?" Tom asked her. His voice sounded different. As though it belonged to someone else. He had a dangerous look in his eyes. Alicia's eyes went wide with fear.

"Why do you have Amanda's diary, Tom?" She asked slowly. Tom didn't say anything. He just kept looking at her. His silence confirmed everything that Alicia feared.

"You killed her, didn't you? She said. "You killed her because she was going to tell Dad and Mia."

"You should not have looked at that diary, Alicia," Tom said in a dangerous voice. "I didn't want to lose both my sisters. But I have no choice now. Yes. Yes, I killed her. I wasn't going to but she kept saying that she'll tell our parents and Mia. I couldn't let that happen. Dad would have kicked me out of office and Mia would have left me. I would have lost everything." He paused. Alicia had forgotten to breathe. Tears were shining in her eyes.

"How could you?" She said. She still could not believe that her brother had killed her sister. "She was your sister."

"Sisters should mind their own business. She didn't and she died. And now you have made the same mistake." He said and took a step forward. Just then, there was a bang and Tom fell to the floor. Alicia saw Mia standing there with a bat in her hands. Her face was wet with tears. Alicia looked at Mia and saw understanding in her eyes.

Tom was handed over to the Police along with Amanda's diary and the recording that Mia had made on her phone of Tom saying that he had killed Amanda.

THE MYSTERY OF MIRANDA'S DEATH

Jon was sitting in a small room with two hard looking Police Officers sitting in front of him with a table between them. Jon had just woken up when these Policemen had arrived at his home and brought him here saying he had killed his girlfriend, Miranda.

"Look, Officers. You must have been mistaken. I don't even know what you guys are talking about," he said, confused. He still couldn't believe that Miranda was dead. He had just dropped her to her home last night. The Policeman, named James, cleared his throat

"Have a look, Jon," he said as he turned the screen of his computer towards Jon. A video was playing there. Jon saw himself take Miranda's hand and walk towards the woods. It must have been a video from a camera in front of a shop. Jon kept on watching. After a while, he saw himself come out of the woods, but this time, he was alone.

"I don't understand," he started, his eyes narrowed in confusion. "I never went into the woods with Miranda. I dropped her in front of her house and watched her go inside. Then I went home." The other Policeman, named Harry, turned the video off and looked at Jon.

"But you see, this video clearly shows that you went back and took her to the woods." He said in a cold voice.

"But, I didn't. I'm telling you I went home," Jon said again. His face was a mix of confusion and worry.

"Do you have any proof of that? Anyone you met who could confirm that?" James asked him.

"No. I didn't meet anyone. I just went home and slept," Jon said slowly. James and Harry just looked at him.

Anna and Bill had come to meet Jon in the cell that he was kept in. They were Jon and Miranda's friends. The two of them were sitting on chairs in front of him. Jon looked sad and worried.

"You guys don't think I killed her, do you?" He asked them in an uncertain tone.

"We don't," Anna replied at once. "We know you loved her." Jon looked a bit relieved.

"The Police have found a video. I don't even know what that video means. It's not true," he was getting emotional.

"Don't worry, mate. We'll find a way," Bill tried to comfort him.

"I hope so," was Jon's only reply.

"Do you think Jon is the killer?" James asked Harry.

"We have the proof here, man. What is there to think about?" Harry said in a light way.

"I don't know. I just think it's strange that he didn't even care about the camera when he took her to the woods. He must have known it was there, wouldn't he?" James said, thinking hard.

"May be he hadn't planned on killing her before. Perhaps he killed her in anger. I don't know. We have the video here," Harry said and got back to his work.

James kept on thinking.

Anna was at Bill's house. This was the 1st time she had come here. Bill had gone to make coffee, leaving her in the sitting room. She got up to look around the house. She opened a door and went inside. The room was small but well organized. The walls were decorated with photos of Bill's favorite singer. Even the cupboard doors had beautiful flowers and butterflies pasted onto them. She went and touched them. The cupboard door was open a bit and Anna saw something inside. Confused, she opened the cupboard.

There, lying on the shelf was Jon's face. No. It was a mask. With Jon's face. Anna didn't understand why the mask had Jon's face. And then it all came to her. Her eyes opened wide in surprise. Just then, there was a sound behind her. She turned. Bill was standing in the doorway. His face looked totally cold.

"Why?" It was all Anna could manage to ask. Bill didn't answer for a while.

"Because you guys are mean," he replied. Anna kept staring at him in confusion.

"Remember how the three of you had made fun of me the first day at college?" Anna remembered that. They had just been having fun with the new student.

"I had decided that day that I would befriend you guys and then destroy you all," Bill said in his cold voice. Anna could not think properly. She had to get out of here. She needed to buy herself time.

"We thought of you as our friend," she said slowly.

"Because I made you think so. You are not my friends. I killed Miranda. Bill is going to jail. And now it's your turn," he said and jumped at her. Anna fell down with a scream. Jon put his knees on her body. With one hand, he covered her mouth so she won't scream and with the other he pushed hard on her neck. Anna couldn't breathe. Bill kept on pushing and pushing. Stars had started to dance in Anna's eyes. She was losing air.

Then, suddenly, the pressure on her neck was released and she took a long breath. She continued to take long breaths until she could breathe properly. When she got up, she saw Bill lying on the floor and Policemen James was standing beside him.

"I had come to ask him a few questions about the case. Seems like I found the killer himself," he said with a smile. Anna couldn't smile. It would take her a while to smile again properly.

THE KILLER'S DIARY

"You should have just stayed quiet," he said in her ears as he pushed the knife further into her body. The girl's eyes went wide with fear and what looked like disbelief. She fell to the ground and after a few moments, went still. He looked at her for a while, then turned around and left.

25 year old Officer Peter Riordan had been called in to look into the case of the girl that had been killed. This was the 5th killing that had ever happened in their small town. All young girls. The 1st girl had been killed 10 years ago. The 2nd, 7 years ago. The 3rd and 4th had been killed within 3 months the same year, 4 years ago. One of them had been Peter's own mother. None of these cases had been solved. This was the reason that had driven Peter to become a Police Officer. He got dressed and went downstairs to the kitchen where his father, Nick Riordan, had prepared breakfast for him. He said good morning to his father, picked up a box of juice and started towards the door.

"Hey, you didn't have breakfast yet," his father called from behind. Peter turned.

"Sorry, Dad. Have to go. It's urgent," he said quickly and went out the door.

At the Police station, a new team had been formed to look in to this case and Peter was to lead this team. The team included him and two other officers named Emma Berenson and Mitch Parker. They had already gathered the basic information about the girl. Her name was Ellery Winston and she was the only daughter of her parents. Her parents had been informed of her death already. Peter and his team headed towards Ellery's home.

The house was just the normal size from the outside but it was beautifully organized inside. Peter, Mitch and Emma were led to the sitting room by a thin blonde woman. She looked to be in her fifties. A man followed her. They all sat down quietly. Peter cleared his throat.

"We are so sorry about your daughter," he said slowly. Mr. and Mrs. Winston didn't say anything.

"We wanted to ask a few things about Ellery, Mr. Winston," Peter went on.

"Call me Tom," Mr. Winston said shortly. "This is Mallory." He said looking at her wife.

"Yes, right. Tom," Peter started. "Can you tell us if Ellery was behaving strange lately?"

"Yes," Mallory spoke suddenly. "Yes, she was. She had gone so quiet and looked worried all the time as if something was going on with her. I asked her what it was a million times but she wouldn't tell me." Mallory had started crying.

"Okay. Did she mention someone? Anyone?" Peter asked her.

"No," she replied softly. They asked a few more questions and then left to meet Ellery's friends.

They met Lacey first. Lacey was Ellery's best friend. She had straight black hair and blue eyes that looked red as blood at the moment.

"So, Lacey. Did Ellery mention anything unusual to you?" Emma asked her. They were all sitting on a sofa in Lacey's home. Lacey thought for a moment.

"No, I don't think so. Although she did seem a bit lost these last few days," Lacey replied.

"She didn't share anything with you?" Mitch asked this time.

"No, not with me at least," she answered.

"Could she have shared with anyone else, then?" Emma asked.

"Simon, perhaps." Lacey said.

"Simon who?" Peter asked.

"Simon is our friend at college. Lacey might have told him something," Lacey replied.

"Wait, Was Simon Lacey's boyfriend?" Emma questioned. Lacey got surprised.

"Oh, no. He is just a friend who was close to Lacey," Lacey started. "And me," she added slowly. "He actually liked Ellery but she didn't like him that way." There was something in Lacey's eyes when she talked about Simon that Peter couldn't quite place. They thanked Lacey and went to meet Simon.

Simon was a thin boy who wore glasses and had brown hair. The three Police Officers were present in his home. He looked jumpy though. Every small sound made him jump.

"Are you okay, Simon?" Emma asked him. Simon looked up.

"Yes. I'm fine," he replied in a low voice.

"Can you tell as anything unusual that you can remember about Lacey?" Peter asked him.

"I don't know. I just saw her yesterday and she was completely fine. I don't know what happened to her," Simon replied at once. The three Officers exchanged a look.

"What do you guys think?" Peter asked Emma and Mitch. They were back in the Police station and were sitting in the office.

"Simon seems odd to me. He liked Ellery, right? She didn't like him back. He might have killed her in anger," Mitch explained his point. Peter looked to Emma.

"What do you say?" He asked her.

"In that way, it could be Lacey too. Did you guys see the look in her eyes when she was talking about Simon?" Emma looked at both of them as she asked. "She is in love with him. But he loved Ellery. Might have tried to get Ellery out of the way," She made her own point. Peter looked at both of them.

"Right. It is possible. But, don't you guys think there could be a relation to the previous 4 killings that happened over the years? I mean the pattern seems the same. Killed with a knife in the woods every time. And the killer has never been caught," Peter made another point. Mitch and Emma didn't say anything. They were thinking.

Nick wasn't around when Peter got home. He went to look for him in the room but he wasn't there. His room looked like he had gone out in a hurry. A diary with a black cover lay on his bed. This was a diary that Peter had seen years ago with his father. And when he had tried to touch it, Nick had told him to stay away from it. Peter went and picked up the diary. He opened a random page.

I killed Stacey today. Peter thought that he had read wrong. So, he read again.

I killed Stacey today. We had been together for a month and she wanted me to marry her or she would tell my wife, Jenna. I had no choice.

Peter couldn't believe his eyes. He opened another page and there was the name of another girl that had been killed. He turned page after page until..............

Jenna found out about my relationship with Ria. She was going to leave me. We were fighting and I pushed her and her head hit the table. She never woke up.

Peter couldn't believe it. There was a page about Ellery too but Peter's mind had stopped working. He was having difficulty believing that his father was a killer who had killed his Mom too. He sat there for some time. At last, he got up and called Mitch. When Nick came home, The Police were waiting for him.

THE MYSTERY MAN

He was hiding in the dark behind the door. He had been waiting for quite some time now. This was not his home. He was waiting for the man to arrive. All his life, Ronan had never killed. He had done other bad things. But, he had never taken anyone's life. Until now. He had been ordered to kill the man who lived in this house.

"You had been trained for this your whole life," the Teacher had told him.

"But who is this man?" He had asked the Teacher.

"No questions until you finish the job," was the reply. So, he had broken into the man's house and had been waiting for him to come. Suddenly, he heard footsteps. The man was coming. Any minute now.

As soon as the door opened, Ronan moved. The man had no time to act until the knife had cut into the side of his body. A painful sound came from the man's mouth. Just then, Ronan looked at the man's face and went still. His eyes opened wide in surprise. The man seemed to notice the same thing on Ronan's face too as he was looking at him in surprise and confusion now. Ronan pulled the knife out and took a step back. The man fell to the floor but was still looking at him. Ronan turned around.

"Wait," he heard the man say. Ronan left. He didn't turn back.

Ronan had grown up almost alone. The Teacher had taken care of him when he was younger but after that, Ronan had to take care of himself. The Teacher came and went whenever he pleased. Ronan was not allowed to ask questions. The Teacher had taught Ronan to steal from and lie to people. But he had not asked him to kill anyone before today. Ronan had spent the day thinking about what had happened with the man. What he had seen. He had a millions lot of questions in his mind at the moment. The Teacher would be coming soon to ask if he had finished his job and Ronan had to prepare an answer before that. But more than that, he wanted to ask the question that had been dancing in his head ever since he had left the man's house.

It was almost midnight when Ronan heard sounds coming from downstairs.

The Teacher must be here. He thought. He dressed up and went downstairs. A middle aged man with brown hair and green eyes was sitting on a chair in the kitchen, drinking from a cup.

"How did it go, boy?" Asked the Teacher before Ronan could reach him. Ronan just stood there for a while.

"I have something to ask you," Ronan said shortly.

"More questions, huh?" The Teacher just kept on drinking from his cup.

"Not that you have answered the previous ones," Ronan said.

"Tell me you killed him and I'll answer your questions," the Teacher said, looking at Ronan. Ronan kept watching him.

"I cut him with the knife. I don't know if he is dead or not," he replied at last.

"Alright. Ask what you want to know," the Teacher offered.

"Why did that man look a lot like me?" Ronan asked at once. The Teacher looked at him with interest.

"Why do you think?" He asked. Ronan did not look away from him.

"Is he……," Ronan could not complete his sentence. The Teacher smiled.

"Yes. He is your father," the Teacher said. "Or was. If he is already dead."

"What?" Ronan's head felt like it was going to break into a thousand pieces. "My father?" He could not believe what he was hearing. Ever since he was young, the Teacher had told him his parents were dead.

"Yes. I stole you from him. He had put me in jail 20 years ago. He is a Policeman you see. My wife died while she was pregnant because I was not there that day to take care of her. I lost everything because of him. I ran from the jail and took you along with me. I had decided that day that I will raise you and then make you kill him," the Teacher explained as he was telling someone else's story. Ronan's disbelief was turning into anger now.

"You……., you made me kill my father," he said at last. His eyes were going red with anger and hatred. "I'll kill you," he said and jumped at the Teacher. The Teacher got away just in time. Ronan ran to catch him again. They kept on fighting for some time until Ronan had him under control. He tied the Teacher to a chair, locked the house and went out. He had to find out about his father.

Ronan found out that his father had been sent to the hospital. He reached the hospital and was so happy to find that his father was alive. His father was also very happy to find his lost son at last.

Ronan turned over the Teacher to the Police. He turned over himself too as he had to pay for the bad things he had done. But, he was happy as he had been reunited with his father.

THE JEWELRY THIEF

It was a bright Saturday morning when Police Officers Rick Nelson and Adam Kelly entered that big house. The report had arrived that Mrs. Hamilton had lost her a million worth of jewelry overnight. They had called in the Police to find the jewelry and catch the thief. The whole family was gathered in the drawing room.

"Hello, Officers. I'm George Hamilton and this is my wife, Rachel," a man who looked in his fifties said while extending a hand and pointing to a woman standing beside him. Rick and Adam shook hands with George and introduced themselves. Then they looked around. Two young boys and a younger girl were present in the room.

"That is Declan, my eldest," George said, pointing to the boy who looked to be around 25 years of age. "And this is Fred." Fred seemed to be around 22 years of age. That left only the girl.

"And that's Daisy, my youngest," George said, looking in the girl's direction. Daisy was definitely in her late teens. They all said their hellos and then sat down.

"Okay, so tell me all that happened last night," Rick asked after they had all settled down.

"Actually, we don't even know what happened," George started. Rick and Adam looked at him.

"The thing is, I had all my jewelry in my drawer. I just saw it last night. And this morning, it wasn't there," Rachel spoke for the first time.

"Yeah, we didn't even hear anything unusual in the night," George added.

"So nothing else was taken?" Adam asked this time.

"No, nothing," George answered. "And another thing is that the house is protected with a lot of alarms. There was no away a thief could have gotten in without the alarms going off." Adam and Rick exchanged a look. The three siblings were silent this whole time.

"Then, perhaps, no one else from the outside came in," Rick said.

"What do you mean?" Rachel asked in confusion.

"What I mean is that if no one came in, it must be someone on the inside," Rick explained.

"What?" George raised his eyebrows.

"We'll need to search the house. The servant rooms first. Can we do that?" Adam asked.

"Oh, I mean, yes. Yes, you can. Although I'm sure you won't find anything. Our servants are very trustworthy," George said. All of them got up and started towards the servant rooms. Rick and Adam went through all the three servant rooms. They kept searching for half an hour but couldn't find anything. At last, they stopped.

"We need to go through all of your rooms too," Rick said looking at the family.

"Sure, by all means," George said and led them towards the rooms. No one seemed to have any problem with it. Only Daisy looked uncomfortable.

Adam and Rick went through George and Rachel's combined bedroom first. This was the room the jewelry had gone missing from. They found nothing out of ordinary in the room. Next, they went through, Fred's room. They looked through his cupboard, drawers and every corner of the room but found nothing.

Next came Daisy's room. It was also searched thoroughly. Nothing found.

"See? I told you, you won't find anything in the house," George said.

"One room remains," Rick said as they entered Declan's room. They searched through his cupboard first but found no jewelry. Then, they opened his drawer and there, sitting in the 2nd drawer was the jewelry box.

"What's this?" Rick said as he picked up the box.

"What? No. That's not possible. I didn't put it there," Declan's voice was full of confusion. Everyone was looking at the jewelry box in surprise. Rachel seemed close to tears.

"Declan, how could you? All my life, ever since I came into this house, I've treated you as my own. I never thought of you as a stepson. And this is how you repay me?" She was looking at Declan with tears in her eyes.

"Mom, no. This is not true. Please," Declan seemed out of words.

"Declan Hamilton, you need to come with us," Rick said to Declan as both him and Adam started guiding me towards the door. Declan looked at his family. No one said anything.

Daisy watched him go with worry in her eyes.

Declan was brought to the Police station for questioning. He was sitting on a chair with Rick and Adam sitting in front of him.

"Look, Declan. We have found a strong proof of your theft in your room. All you have to do is agree to it," Adam said to Declan.

"I have told you so many times before and I'll say this again that I do not know how it got there. I did not steal the jewelry," Declan said angrily. Adam and Rick just looked at each other.

"Do you think I would have just left it in my drawer for everyone to see?" Declan said again, looking at them. Adam and Rick just exchanged a look but didn't reply.

Daisy was sitting on her bed in her room. She was thinking hard. She seemed to be trying to make some kind of a decision. At last, she stood up and walked to her parents' room. She knocked and went inside.

"Mom, Dad. I need to tell you something," she told her parents. They looked up at her.

"What is it, Daisy?" Her mother asked lovingly.

"It wasn't Declan who stole your jewelry," she said, at last.

"What?" Her mother asked, confused.

"What do you mean, Daisy?" Her father asked this time.

"It was Fred. I saw him. Look," she said and handed them her cell phone where she had taken a photo of Fred holding the jewelry box. Her parents looked at the photo in surprise.

"Why didn't you say so before?" His father asked.

"I thought he was just doing a joke or something. That's why I took the photo. I didn't know he was going to put it in Declan's room," Daisy was crying now. "I'm so sorry." She said through tears. George's face had hardened. Rachel seemed at loss for words.

"I'm going to call the Police," George said as he picked up his phone.

Fred was questioned by the Police and he admitted to his theft at last. He told them that he had tried to frame Declan so that their father won't trust Declan again and he himself would get all the shares in the company. His parents were really disappointed in him.

Declan was free and the jewelry thief had been caught at last.

WHO KILLED ALBERT?

He was lying on the floor, his eyes open in disbelief and his shirt wet with blood. A person dressed all in black was standing beside him, holding a knife. It was red with blood.

"You should rest now. You've lived enough," the person said and kept on looking at the man lying on the floor until his body went still. The person then disappeared.

It was a holiday center called Rose. Police Officer Arya Miller had arrived with Officer Robert Peterson.

"Who is the manager of this place? She asked.

"Here. I'm Emilia Carter, the manager. I called you," a woman answered.

"You are the one who found the body? Arya asked.

"Yes. I found the body of Albert Greyson in the storage room this morning and immediately called you," replied Emilia. Arya looked around.

"And who are these people?" She asked, looking at the other four people. Two girls and two boys.

"They are Albert's friends. All of them came here to spend their holidays together two days ago," replied Emilia. Arya looked at them closely. All four of them looked like they had been crying. Their eyes looked reddish. One of the girls was still crying.

"So you guys are his friends," she said, looking at them.

"Yes, I'm Bill. This is Mitchell, my girlfriend and that's Erwin," said one of the boys.

"And that's Nina, Al's girlfriend," he went on, pointing at the crying girl.

"Right. So what do you guys think? Who could have killed Albert?" Arya asked, looking from one to the other.

"We have no idea," said Mitchell.

"Where were all of you last night?" Arya asked.

"The girls shared one room and we three boys shared the other. Last night, I was on the roof with Mitchell and Erwin was in the room. Then later, I went back to the room and Al was still not there. We thought he would be with Nina. But we got worried when he didn't return even after midnight. So Erwin and I went to check on him. We went to the girls' room and Nina was there. She said she hadn't seen him since evening. We looked for him everywhere but couldn't find him. And then he was found in the storage room in the morning," Bill explained. Arya thought for a while.

"Did he get into a fight with someone here?" She asked. Everyone started to think.

"Yes. In fact, he did. Just last afternoon," said Erwin, remembering something. Arya's eyes brightened.

"With whom?" She asked quickly.

"I think his name was William Carsen. He is also a guest here. He was hitting on Nina so Albert hit him in the face," replied Erwin. Arya turned to Emilia.

"Where is he? We would like to meet him," she said. Emilia turned to walk away.

Arya Miller and Peterson were sitting with William Carsen in front of them. Arya studied him for a while.

"Mr. Carsen, we have come to know that you got into a fight with Albert Greyson last afternoon for hitting on his girlfriend?" She asked him.

"Yes," he replied.

"And you must be aware of the fact that Mr. Greyson has been killed last night," she went on.

"Are you saying that I killed him?" He said, surprised.

"We are just doing what we have to do, Mr. Carsen and you must know that the fact that you fought with him the same day puts you in a very difficult position," Arya said, looking at him closely.

"I did get into a small fight with him. But why would I go and kill him for such a small thing?" he said. Arya watched him for a while.

"Alright, Mr. Carsen. You may go for now," she said and sat back on her chair.

"What do you think, Robert?" She asked officer Peterson after William had left.

"I'm not sure yet, boss. We'll have to find out more," he replied.

It had been three days. All the guests were not allowed to leave the place until the killer was caught. Nina was sitting at a bench, looking at the moon. Erwin came and put his jacket around her shoulders.

"You'll catch a cold," he said, sitting down. She did not say anything. He looked at her. She was crying. He put an arm around her shoulders.

"It'll be alright," he said. She rested her head on his shoulder and cried.

Arya and Peterson were sitting in the office. Arya was looking at the photos of the guests in Paradise that she had attached on a board on the wall. She was thinking. Peterson was going through some files.

"The knife that the killer used to kill Albert is still not found," she said slowly.

"Yes. We have already searched the area around the building," Peterson replied.

"We need to search again," she said and got up to leave. Peterson followed her quickly.

"Isn't this Erwin's jacket?" Mitchell asked Nina.

"Yeah. I forgot to give it back to him," Nina replied. The door of their room opened and Bill entered.

"Come on guys. Let's go have lunch," he said.

"You guys go ahead. I'm coming," Nina said. Both of them left. Nina got up and was just going to put the jacket away when she felt something in the pocket.

Arya was back in her office. She was waiting for Peterson. They had found a knife hidden in the ground behind the building and she had sent it for blood tests. She was just going to call him when he entered the room.

"Boss, the test results have arrived," he said, excitedly.

"And?" She asked, waiting for the answer.

"We have found the blood of two people on it. Albert must have fought the killer before dying, cutting him somehow," he replied. Arya's eyes brightened.

Nina was looking at the watch in her hands with wide eyes. Just then, Erwin entered the room. Nina looked at him with disbelief in her eyes.

"This is the watch that I gave to Al. What is this doing in your jacket Erwin?" She asked him. Her eyes were shining with tears. She was looking at him in shock. He did not say anything.

"Did you.... Did you kill him?" She asked again. Her eyes were wide with fear and disbelief. Erwin looked at her for a while and then took a step forward. She moved backwards.

"You have to listen to me, Nina," he said slowly.

"No! Stay away from me. How could you, Erwin? How could you?" She was crying now. Her face was wet with tears.

"It was because of you. Why did he have to come between us? I love you, Nina. We have known each other since childhood. How could you choose him over me?" He said in a mad way. Nina looked at him surprise. He seemed to be out of control. Nina did not know what to do. He came closer and put his hand on her cheek.

Just then, the door opened and Officer Arya Miller entered with a gun pointed at Erwin.

"Put your hands up," she said to him. Erwin looked at her and then ran to the window. He was going to climb out but Detective Peterson was standing just outside the window with two other Policemen. Erwin was caught and taken away. He was screaming and calling out to Nina as they were pulling him away.

Arya came to Nina and put a hand on her arm.

"It's all over now," she said and put a hand on her shoulder as she cried.

THE END